To Dr. M. J. Smith, with thanks ~ C. F.

For Doreen and family, with love ~ B. C.

ALADDIN

An imprint of Simon & Schuster Children's Publishing Division

1230 Avenue of the Americas, New York, NY 10020

First Aladdin hardcover edition May 2015

Text copyright © 2014 by Claire Freedman

Illustrations © 2014 by Ben Cort

Originally published in Great Britain in 2014 by Simon and Schuster UK, Ltd.

All rights reserved, including the right of reproduction in whole or in part in any form.

ALADDIN is a trademark of Simon & Schuster, Inc., and related logo is a

registered trademark of Simon & Schuster, Inc.

For information about special discounts for bulk purchases, please contact

Simon & Schuster Special Sales at 1-866-506-1949 or business@simonandschuster.com.

The Simon & Schuster Speakers Bureau can bring authors to your live event.

For more information or to book an event contact the Simon & Schuster Speakers Bureau

at 1-866-248-3049 or visit our website at www.simonspeakers.com.

Designed by Karina Granda

Manufactured in China 0215 SUK

2 4 6 8 10 9 7 5 3 1

This book has been cataloged with the Library of Congress

ISBN 978-1-4814-4252-7 (hc)

ISBN 978-1-4814-4253-4 (eBook)

Monsters Love Underpants

ILLUSTRATED BY
Ben Cort

CLAIRE FREEDMAN

aladdin
NEW YORK   LONDON   TORONTO   SYDNEY   NEW DELHI

Monsters think it's MONSTER fun,
to creep around, all scary!
But there's something they love even MORE,
than looking mean and hairy!

Monsters all LOVE underpants,
     and think pants are fun-tastic.
They like all patterns, shapes, and styles,
     and twanging pants elastic!

Some prowl through dingy dungeons: "Oooooow!"
You hear them howling, loudly.
CREAK! One finds squeaky armour pants,
    and clanks around SO proudly!

Drool monsters from the steamy swamp,
    fill pants with gooey slime.
But, OOOOPS! Their pants get slippery,
    and slide down all the time!

Wild, woolly mountain monsters
make explorers faint with fright!
CLOMP! They snatch their frozen pants,
then run off in the night!

At the bottom of the ocean,
a pirate ship now rests,
Where sea monsters wear pants with jewels
they've pinched from treasure chests!

The spiky, spooky, space monsters

all wave and roar, "Hooray!"

When out from blackest, deepest space,

bright bloomers float their way!

It's not the sand inside his pants
        that makes this monster twitchy.
His underpants are way too small.
"I wish they weren't so itchy!"

It's Saturday—their Disco Night.

They wear pants bold and brave.

The password (sshh!) is WOBBLY PANTS.

to get inside the cave.

The monsters show their pants off
as they dance the Monster Bop.
Their pants-clad bottoms jig and jive,
till someone yells out, "STOP!"

"It's almost daylight! Quick, back home . . .
we can't risk being spotted!
For no one will be scared of us
in pants all striped and dotted!"

So if you hear strange scuffles
    from beneath your bed—
    beware!
You might just catch a monster
    trying on YOUR
    snazzy pair!